DAN'S DEN

Piccadilly Pips

DAN'S DEN

Ian Strachan
Illustrated by Lucy Su

Piccadilly Press • London

Ian Strachan lives in Eccles Hall, Staffordshire. When he was Dan's age he, like Dan, lived in a town, but his holidays were spent at his gran's in the country. She kept hens and bees and grew her own vegetables. There was a patch of rough ground where he and his brother built a den, but the only visitors they had were flies, ants and the odd hen!
Ian Strachan's best known books are: MOSES BEECH (winner of the Young Observer Teenage Fiction Prize), THROWAWAYS (winner of the Wirral Library Paperback Award) and THE BOY IN THE BUBBLE (winner of the Federation of Children's Book Groups Book of the Year, among other prizes).

Lucy Su lives in Kew with her husband and two daughters, Beatrice and Olivia. She has done a large variety of illustration work but her growing interest in children's illustration was boosted by having her own to help with test runs!

Phototypeset from author's disk by Piccadilly Press.
Printed and bound in India by Thomson Press
for the publishers Piccadilly Press Ltd.,
5 Castle Road, London NW1 8PR

A catalogue record for this book is available from the British Library
ISBNs: 1 85340 457 8 (hardback)   1 85340 452 7 (paperback)

ONE

On his hands and knees, Dan
crawled slowly through the Jungle.
Summer sunlight drifted down
through the trees and tangled under-
growth above him. As he moved,
Dan listened out for the slightest
sound of the enemy. Grass seeds
dropped down the back of his
striped T-shirt, making him itch.
Thorns scratched his bare arms, but
Dan kept going towards his goal.

Suddenly the grass to Dan's right parted. A small black and white dog burst out into the open and began to bark at Dan.

"Shut up!" Dan hissed. Knowing that the dog would give him away, he made a grab for its collar, but missed.

Seconds later, a voice called out from a branch above Dan, "You might as well come out. I know you're there."

Dan got to his feet, grumbling at the dog, "That was all your fault! I'd never have been caught if you hadn't given me away."

The dog simply wagged its tail.

A boy, wearing faded jeans and a blue T-shirt, jumped down beside Dan. He had very short dark hair and a broad grin on his face. "Dan, it's no use blaming Smudge. I knew

where you were all the time.
Anyway, it's my turn now. Cover
your eyes while I hide and, this time,
no cheating."

Dan scowled, picked up a stick and
swung it about him, knocking seed
heads off the head-high grass. "I'm
fed up with this game, Josh."

For the first time in ages, the smile on Josh's face faded. "That's not fair. You weren't fed up when it was your turn to hide."

"I'm sick of playing the same old games," Dan said. "I want to do something different."

Josh tilted his head to one side. "Like what?"

"Oh, I don't know," Dan confessed.

There were five more weeks of the summer holidays left and the two friends were already bored. The Jungle, their name for the overgrown patch of waste ground which ran along the backs of the houses on the edge of town, was their special place. As well as being the Jungle, sometimes Dan and Josh pretended they were struggling across the Sahara desert. In winter, if snow fell, then they became explorers, battling to reach the North Pole – although Smudge refused to pull their sledge.

Dan's eyes suddenly lit up. "I know! Let's build a den. We've always said we would, but never got round to it."

Josh forgot all about losing his turn to hide. "Okay! But where?"

Dan and Josh thought hard. They both knew every bush and tree of the Jungle.

Josh suggested, "We could build it down by the pool."

Dan shook his head. "It gets too wet round there when it rains. What about the fallen tree?"

With Josh and Smudge close behind him, Dan ran towards the old, dead tree on the edge of the Jungle which had blown down during a winter gale. Sandy soil still clung to its upturned roots and the scarred trunk was overgrown with nettles and brambles.

Using his stick, Dan beat a path through the weeds. Soon they were sitting underneath the base of the trunk, behind green curtains of plants and shrubs.

"This is great!" Josh said, stretching out full-length on the ground. "All we need do is get some more grass and branches to hide the entrance. Nobody will ever find us in here."

"Maybe not in the summer," Dan agreed, looking about him, "but what about in the winter, when all the weeds die down? It would be better if we could use it all year."

"But we'll never be able to keep the rain out," Josh said.

"We'll have to think of something." Smudge, who had fallen asleep, suddenly pricked up his ears and barked. "What is it, Smudge?" Dan asked. Then they heard Dan's mother calling him in for tea.

They scrambled out of the tunnel and leapt over tussocks of grass. Whilst jogging home, Dan said, "See you back at our Den straight after tea."

Josh grinned, "Okay."

Dan added, "And bring anything you can find which might be useful."

The two friends parted by the fence at the bottom of Dan's garden. Dan swung two loose planks back and then followed Smudge through the gap.

TWO

Dan's father was working in the garden. He was laying bricks around three sides of a large concrete slab. When the walls and roof were finished, it would be a garage.

He used his trowel to "butter" a brick with mortar and then dropped it neatly into place. "That's the last one for now," Dad said. He rinsed off the trowel blade in a bucket of water. "Come on, Dan, tea's waiting."

Dan followed his father, but he tripped over something half hidden by the pile of sand. At first it looked like the corner of a plastic sack – the kind Dad used for bringing sand home from the builder's yard.

"Had a good trip?" Dad asked, laughing at his silly joke.

But Dan, thinking a sack might come in handy for keeping things dry in their Den, tugged at the plastic. As Dan pulled, he found it was not a sack after all, but a great long length of clear, green plastic.

"What's this for?" Dan asked.

"That's left over from the sheet I put under the concrete to keep the damp out of the garage floor," Dad explained.

"Can I have it?" Dan asked eagerly.

Dad looked puzzled. "What do you want that for?"

"To use as a ground-sheet."

"But, Dan, you haven't got a tent!" Dad said.

"I might have, one day. Please, can I have it? *Please*?"

"Oh, I suppose so," Dad agreed. "But don't leave it lying around in the garden, or I'll take it back."

"I promise," Dan said. "I'll take it out of the garden straight after tea."

By the time Smudge and Dan arrived at the Den with the plastic sheet, Josh was already standing beside the tree with two milk crates. "I thought these would do for seats. What's that you've got?"

"A cover to go over the tree and keep the rain out," Dan explained.

It took nearly an hour of hard work to clear all the weeds away from the tree. Then they threw the sheet over the trunk and weighted the edges down with stones.

Finally, as they hid the sheet by draping the weeds and some other branches over the sides, Dan said, "New weeds will soon grow back over it."

"Come on," Josh said, "let's go inside and try it."

Smudge, who was enjoying the new game, led the way. "Smudge! This isn't your new kennel," Dan said, "it's *our* Den."

Inside, when they were sitting on the crates, Dan grinned with pride. "This is really great! The plastic will keep all the wind and rain out. It's so warm, we could even sleep out here."

Josh shook his head. "I don't think my mum would let me."

"Nor mine," Dan agreed. "Besides, we'd have to ask and I want to keep the Den as our secret."

For the next few days, the Den was the centre for all their games. While they were being explorers, it was their jungle hide. When they became trappers, it became the offices of the Hudson Bay Company, where they traded furs for food. They camped out in it on the surface of the moon and, another time, it was an underwater cave.

Each day, they brought more things to make the Den more comfortable. Mostly it was stuff from their own rooms, but sometimes they found old things lying around. Josh brought a travel rug and two old

cushions, which he found in the loft, to put on top of the crates. Dan rescued a wobbly coffee table from a rubbish skip.

"It's getting so good," Dan said, "we could almost live in here now."

But one morning, as they got close to the Den, instead of rushing in as usual, Smudge just stood by the entrance, barking. Not only that, but the curtain of grass and weeds, which the boys always left to hide the opening, had been thrown aside.

Josh was shocked, "Somebody's been in our den!"

"And by the way Smudge is barking," Dan added, "whoever it was, is still in there."

The two crept to the doorway and carefully peered inside.

"Hello boys!" The croaky sound of a man's voice came from the back of the Den. As their eyes got used to the dim light, Dan and Josh saw an old man sitting on a crate.

He reminded Dan a little of his grandad, who had died last year. Dan still missed him very much.

This old man had a round, red face and a few tufts of white hair, which sprang up around the edges of his mostly bald head.

But, even in the gloom, his most striking feature was a pair of bright blue eyes. They sparkled as he said, "I was wondering when someone would turn up."

"What are you doing in here?" Josh demanded.

"This is *our* Den!" Dan said firmly.

"Oh, don't worry," the man said. "I won't steal it! But last night, I was looking for somewhere to sleep and I came across this place, so I stayed. I must say, you've made it very snug."

Josh looked at the man's worn shoes, grubby trousers and stained, short-sleeved shirt. "Are you a tramp?"

The old man laughed. "No, of course not!"

"Then why didn't you sleep in your own house?" Dan asked.

For a moment the man's eyes lost all their glitter. Then he said brightly, "I just thought I'd like a change. But I'm very hungry. I don't suppose either of you have got anything to eat, have you?"

Dan shook his head. From his pocket, Josh pulled the crumpled end of a tube of mints. "This is all I've got."

The man took all the mints, popped three in his mouth and stuffed the rest into his shirt pocket. As he sucked them, he said, "They're better than nothing. Do you live round here then?" The boys nodded. "Then maybe," the old man suggested, "when you go in for your dinners, you could bring me something back?"

Dan looked startled. "You mean, you're going to stay here?"

The man laughed loudly. "I think I will. Just for a while. If that's all right with you?"

It wasn't, but Dan and Josh were too polite to say so. They just nodded.

THREE

"What do they call you two?" the old man asked.

Josh and Dan told him and then Dan asked, "What's your name?"

Another slightly puzzled look briefly clouded the old man's eyes, before he replied, "You can call me Bob. So, now what are we going to do?"

The two boys looked at each other. Because a slight wind had got up, they had talked about pretending the Den was the bridge of a ship. But they could not do that with a grown-up hanging about.

"I know," Bob suddenly said, "why don't we play hide and seek?"

"Okay," the boys reluctantly agreed.

The old man suggested, "I'll be on first. You two go and hide, while I count to a hundred."

Knowing the Jungle as well as they did, the two quickly found a brilliant hiding place together. They crouched down inside a patch of brambles and waited.

"Do you think Bob's going to stay in our Den for long?" Josh asked.

"I hope not," Dan replied.

Minutes ticked away, but there was no sign of the old man.

"I think there's something a bit odd about him," Dan muttered.

"What sort of *odd*?"

"Well, for a start," Dan said, "I don't think Bob is his real name. I think he made it up. In fact, I think he's on the run."

Josh gaped at Dan, "You mean he's a criminal?"

Dan shrugged. "I don't know, but

we ought to find out."

Ages passed, with still no sign of the old man. The boys were getting fed up with waiting.

"He'll never find us," Dan said. "Let's go back."

When they got to the Den, Bob was sitting there and looked as if he had never moved.

Dan was cross. "You were supposed to be looking for us."

"Oh, yes, I know that," Bob said.

"Then why didn't you?" Josh demanded.

Before Bob could answer, Dan asked, "Are you hiding from somebody yourself? Is that why you're here?"

"Well, sort of," Bob agreed.

"Are you on the run?" Josh asked.

"Have you committed a terrible crime?" Dan wondered.

The old man laughed. "No, of course not. But I can see I can't hide anything from two bright young lads like you. I'd better tell you the truth. Although I've done nothing wrong, there are people after me. If they catch me, they'll lock me away."

"Gosh!" Dan whispered.

Seeing how impressed the boys were, Bob added, "Or, worse still, my life could be in danger."

"That's awful!" Josh gasped.

Dan asked, "Are you some sort of secret agent?"

Bob raised a finger to his lips. "Sssh! You never know who might hear us! This must be our secret. You've got to promise you won't tell anyone I'm here. Not even your parents. Promise?"

Wide-eyed, the two boys whispered, "We promise!"

Now they had two huge secrets – their Den and Bob! They were thrilled to be part of a real-life adventure instead of just another of their make-believe games.

Bob said hopefully, "Do think it's getting anywhere near lunchtime? Because I'm starving!" Then he added in a hushed whisper, "But remember, not a word about me, or any of this, to your parents!"

FOUR

"Dan," his mother was busy searching the fridge, "have you seen the remains of that pork pie we had for tea yesterday?"

Dan shifted uneasily from foot to foot. The cold piece of pie was making an uncomfortable bulge under his sweatshirt. "Maybe Smudge ate it," he suggested.

His mother glanced at Smudge, who wagged his tail, sniffed at Dan's sweatshirt and barked.

Mum said, "Don't be silly! Smudge couldn't get into the fridge. Not unless somebody left the door open."

"Dad might have eaten it."

Mum shook her head. "That pork pie isn't the first thing I've missed. Leftovers keep disappearing." She looked closely at Dan. "Are you having another growth spurt?"

Dan, feeling very uncomfortable, forced a grin. "Maybe I've started walking in my sleep. I could be raiding the fridge without even knowing it. Look, Mum, I've got to go, or I'll be late meeting Josh!"

As Dan climbed out through the fence, he was still worrying about what he had just said to his mother. Although he had not lied, he had not told the whole truth.

When he had first started taking

odd scraps of food for Bob, it had not seemed so bad. Dan told himself it was only like having an extra helping, but then finding you could not quite manage to finish it.

But, over the next two weeks, things got worse. They quickly found out that, for somebody who simply sat around all the time, Bob had a huge appetite. Hardly had he eaten breakfast before he was asking if it was time for lunch. It almost seemed as if he did not remember he had only just eaten. One way or another, Bob was asking non-stop for food.

"Why don't you go down to the shops and buy something?" Dan asked him.

Bob shrugged and began to get to his feet. "Okay, Dan, if that's what you want. But don't bother going to the police if I don't come back. It's just that THEY will have got me!"

"No, you're right," Dan sighed.
"We can't risk you being seen. We'll
manage somehow."

"Good, lad!" Bob said, slapping Dan on the back. "I knew you two wouldn't let me down. Oh, and do you think you could get me a bigger bottle of lemonade next time? My mouth's as dry as a desert."

But in spite of that problem, plus sometimes getting in the way, Dan had mostly enjoyed having the old man around. Bob was full of ideas. He had shown them how to fold proper paper aeroplanes and he had made them a brilliant kite, which he cut out of a plastic carrier bag. In many ways, the last couple of weeks had almost been as good as having Grandad back again.

Crossing the Jungle, Dan, still clutching the pork pie under his sweatshirt, caught up with Josh. He told him that Mum was asking difficult questions about all the food he was taking.

Josh replied, "But it's not stealing. Not when we're only taking things from our own houses."

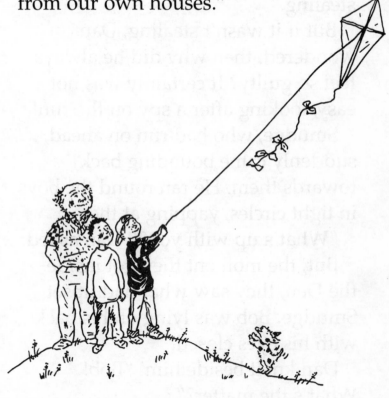

"Isn't it?" Dan asked. They certainly did not have anyone's permission to take the food.

"Of course not," Josh said firmly. "It's not like taking stuff from shops without paying. That really would be stealing."

But if it wasn't stealing, Dan wondered, then why did he always feel so guilty? It certainly was not easy, looking after a spy on the run!

Smudge, who had run on ahead, suddenly came bounding back towards them. He ran round the boys in tight circles, yapping at them.

"What's up with you?" Dan asked.

But, the moment they got inside the Den, they saw what had upset Smudge. Bob was lying on his back with his eyes closed.

Dan knelt beside him. "Bob! What's the matter?"

But although Bob moaned slightly, his eyes stayed shut and he did not reply.

"He must be very ill," Dan said.

"You don't think THEY found him and slipped poison into his drink, do you?" asked Josh.

"I don't know, but he's very ill," Dan said. He stood up. "We'll have to get help. I'll go and tell Mum."

Josh grabbed Dan's arm. "We can't do that! Bob made us promise we wouldn't tell anybody about him hiding here."

"But he wasn't sick then," Dan pointed out.

Josh looked worried. "But remember what he said – if they find him, they might kill him."

"If we don't get some help, he could die anyway!"

"But it'll mean everyone will know about the Den."

"It can't be helped," Dan said.

"And we'll have to own up about taking the food."

The thought of being shouted at by Mum made Dan pause for a second. Then he remembered the people who had tried to help Grandad when he was ill. Although they had not succeeded, at least they had tried.

"We must do something," Dan said, firmly. "Whatever happens to us, Bob's ill and we've got to get help. Are you coming?"

Josh looked at the ill man and then thought about being shouted at by Dan's mum. "I think I'll stay here and look after Bob."

With Smudge snapping at his heels, Dan bounded back to the

house. He raced up the garden and burst into the kitchen.

"Mum, there's a man in our Den, in the Jungle. He's very poorly and I think he's going to die!"

Mum looked startled. "Now, Dan, calm down! I don't understand what you're saying. Tell me again, slowly."

Dan took a deep breath. This time he managed to get the whole story out. When he had finished, Dan expected his mother to start telling him off. Instead she went straight to the hall and phoned for an ambulance.

When she put down the phone, Dan asked timidly, "Aren't you cross?"

"There'll be time to talk about all that later," Mum said.

She quickly found an old blanket, grabbed a bottle of water and together they set off across the Jungle.

FIVE

"Are the sausages done yet?" Dan asked.

They were sizzling on a grill over the campfire, which glowed bright red in the evening light. Dan's mum and dad, together with Josh's mum, had all joined the boys. They were sitting on rugs outside the Den. During the afternoon they had visited the old man again. He had been in hospital for four days and, though much better, he was still recovering from his heart attack.

"The sausages are nearly ready," Dad said, giving them a final turn.

Dan thought it felt strange, being at the Den without the old man. "I'm sorry he wasn't really a spy on the run."

Dad pointed out, "The police *were* looking for him."

"Yes," Dan agreed. "But only

because he'd wandered off from the old folks' home."

"I'll never get used to calling him George!" Josh said.

"Do you think he really didn't know his own name, or where he lived?" Dan asked.

His mother smiled. "People can get very mixed up about things as they get older."

"Will we still be able to go and see George, when he goes back to live at The Cedars?" Josh asked.

Josh's mother said, "I'm sure he'd like that. They say he doesn't usually get any visitors. He probably only wandered off to look for some company."

Dan's mum pointed out, "And if it wasn't for you two boys, I'm not sure George would still be alive today."

"It was just as well we broke our

promise to him," Dan sighed.

Dad said sternly, "It would have been better if you'd never made that kind of promise in the first place."

"And then I wouldn't have worried about all the disappearing food," his mother said.

"Sorry," Dan said.

"Me too," Josh nodded.

"Secrets are all very well," his father said, "but they can sometimes be very dangerous. Now, come on, everyone! The sausages are done, so eat up!"

Dan bit deeply into the roll which held the fat, juicy sausage and decided this was the best meal he had ever eaten! And, although the Den was no longer a secret, Dan decided that sharing it was going to be even more fun.